Hop Aboard! Here We Go!

We go by car
    And we go by train,
We go by boat
    And we go by plane.

We go by land
    And sea and air,
We go, go, go,
    From here to there.

GO, GO, GO!

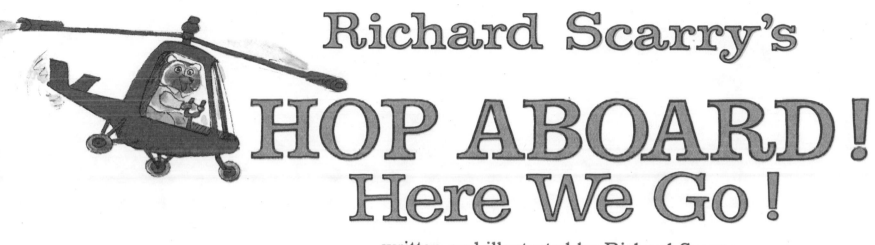

Richard Scarry's
HOP ABOARD!
Here We Go!

written and illustrated by Richard Scarry

GOLDEN PRESS • NEW YORK
Western Publishing Company, Inc.
Racine, Wisconsin

Cars,
Busses,
and
Trucks

Here are Roger and Flip, out for
a ride in their convertible.

When Flip is in a hurry,
he always takes a taxi.

The mail truck delivers the mail.
Do you have a letter for me,
Mailman Roger?

Policeman Roger cruises the streets
in his patrol car to make sure
that there is no trouble.

Would you like to ride in the top of a double-decker bus?
Hop aboard then, and see the sights of the city.

Vrrroooomm! Roger and Flip roar around the race track in their racing car. I hope they win, don't you?

The delivery motorcycle is carrying a small package from the store to the customer's house.

This big trailer truck is carrying a heavy load of books from the printing plant to the store. Roger and Flip like to read books when they're not working.

Roger the telephone man is going to put a new telephone in Flip's house. Do you like to talk on the telephone?

The garbage truck grumbles and growls, packing the garbage inside. When it is full, off it rumbles to the dump.

There's room for lots of friends in Roger's station wagon. You can come, too. Hop aboard!

A pickup truck is handy to have on a farm. "It sure holds a lot of chickens," says Flip.

There's just room for Roger and Flip in this speedy little sports car.

Fire Chief Roger whizzes to fires in his red fire chief's car.

The school bus takes the pupils to school and brings them home again in the afternoon. My, the pupils look wide awake this morning!

The auto carrier delivers new cars to the showroom.
Flip has already picked out the car he wants.

The concrete mixer's drum grinds around
and around, mixing the concrete on the way
to the job. What do you think Roger and
Flip are going to build with all that concrete?

The little drugstore car delivers
medicines to people's homes, to help
them feel better fast.

Cowboy Roger and his sidekick Flip drive their cattle
to a greener pasture in the livestock truck.

Whoops! The dump truck tips up,
and Flip gets tipped out.

Bumpety, bumpety, bump. The sturdy
jeep can go almost anywhere. Up hill
or down, through sand or mud, it never
gets stuck.

The big gasoline tanker delivers
gas to the filling station.

Rattle, clank! Here comes the milk
truck, delivering bottles of milk.

This truck delivers crates
of soft drinks to stores.

This rescue truck can go on land or water. Silly Flip was swimming too far out, and Roger had to rescue him.

Ring-a-ling. Here comes the ice-cream truck. What flavor ice cream would you like, Flip?

The motor scooter goes put-put-put down the street. Hold on tight, Flip!

The motorcycle policeman chases after speeding cars.

Big busses carry many passengers and all their luggage. Sometimes they go all the way across the country. Flip is taking a cross-country trip for his vacation.

Don't fall off that ladder, Flip!

When a house catches on fire, the brave fire
brigade rushes to the rescue, sirens shrieking.
Don't worry, they will put out the fire.

The hook-and-ladder is so long that it needs
two drivers, one to steer the front and one to
steer the back. The firemen use the long ladder
to rescue people and to get closer to fires
in tall buildings.

*Puss! Get out of that burning
house this instant!*

The pumper truck pumps water
from the hydrant through the long hose.

The ambulance will take anyone
who is hurt to the hospital.

This old-time electric taxi
ran on batteries. The
driver sat in the back.

This truck is used to carry
baggage and tired dogs around
a railroad station.

Flip and Roger are on an expedition to
the South Pole. Their snow tractor's
treads crunch over the snow and ice.

The strong trailer truck carries
this heavy power shovel from job
to job. I wonder if Flip's getting
ready to dig up some old bones?

Old station wagons had sides of beautiful polished wood.

Roger and Flip scoot along in their old-time "Tin Lizzie," enjoying the breeze and the fresh air.

The airport bus takes pilots and passengers from the city to the airport.

The big logging trailer hauls logs from the forest to the sawmill, where they are cut into boards.

Oh dear, Flip has had a wreck.
Roger's tow truck tows the car to
the garage for repairs.

The children sing "Mary Had a
Little Lamb" as the happy little
nursery school bus takes them
to nursery school.

This old-fashioned car has a
rumble seat in the back
to carry extra friends.

Flip uses his large, comfortable town
car when he is in the big city. "To
the circus," he tells his chauffeur.

Zzzipp! There go Roger and Flip
in their dandy red sports car.

Here comes the big snowplow, clearing
snow from the roads and spreading
sand on the slippery spots.

The back of the high-lift dump truck
rises high up to dump its load.
Look out, Flip!

People who live in a house trailer can take their home along
as they travel about the country.

But, do you think
Flip's little car can pull
that big heavy trailer?

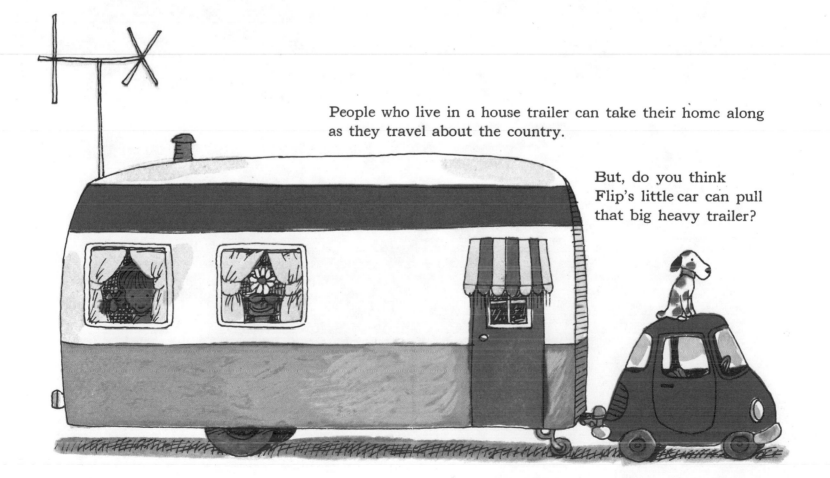

Airplanes,
Aircraft,
and
Spacecraft

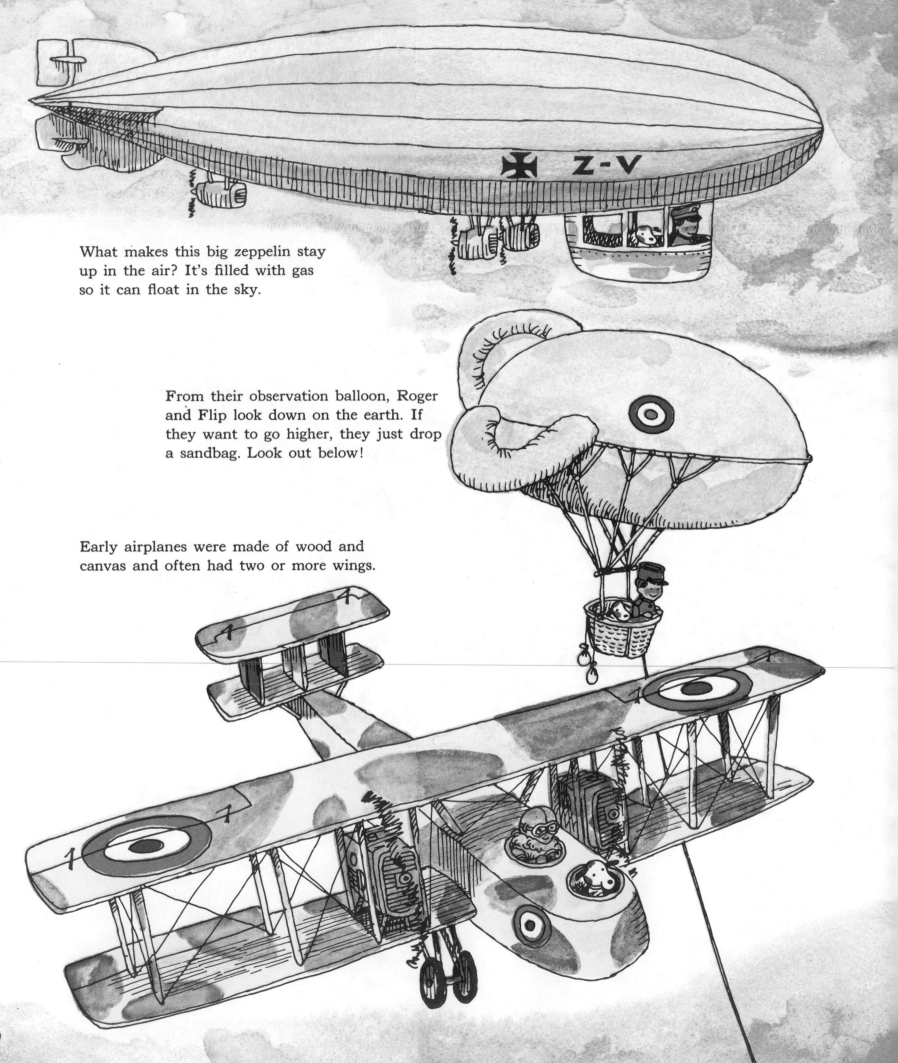

What makes this big zeppelin stay up in the air? It's filled with gas so it can float in the sky.

From their observation balloon, Roger and Flip look down on the earth. If they want to go higher, they just drop a sandbag. Look out below!

Early airplanes were made of wood and canvas and often had two or more wings.

Some Early Planes

A monoplane was an old-time plane with only one wing.

A plane with three wings was called a triplane.

Here are Roger and Flip looping the loop in a *Spad* biplane, a plane with two wings.

Zzzzooommm. There go Roger and Flip in a speedy *Albatross*.

Roger and Flip fly over enemy territory in their French observation plane. What maneuvers are the troops planning?

Vrooommm. There they go again, this time in a *Sopwith Camel*.

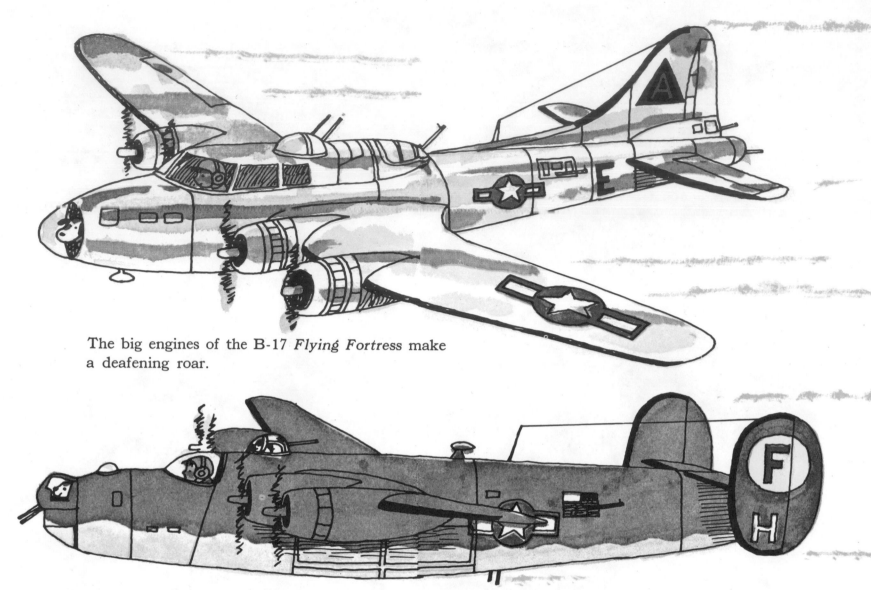

The big engines of the B-17 *Flying Fortress* make a deafening roar.

The B-24 *Liberator* rumbles through the sky.

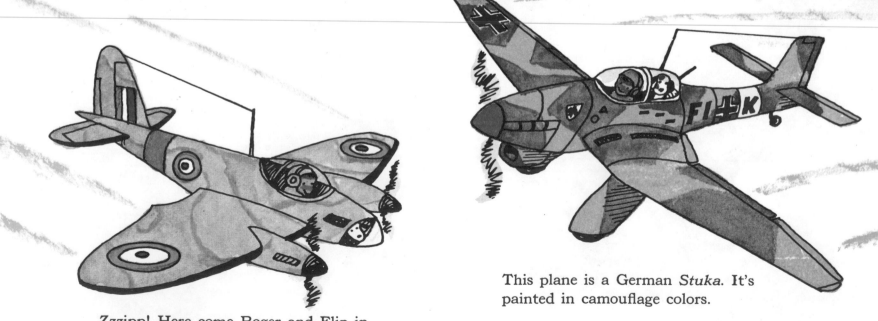

Zzzipp! Here come Roger and Flip in a fast little plane called the *Mosquito*.

This plane is a German *Stuka*. It's painted in camouflage colors.

This P-38 *Lightning* looks as if it could eat its way through the clouds with those sharp teeth.

The camouflage on this *Messerschmitt* 109 makes it look like a flying leopard.

Down dive Roger and Flip in their speedy *Spitfire*.

Roger and Flip climb high into the sky in their P-51 *Mustang*.

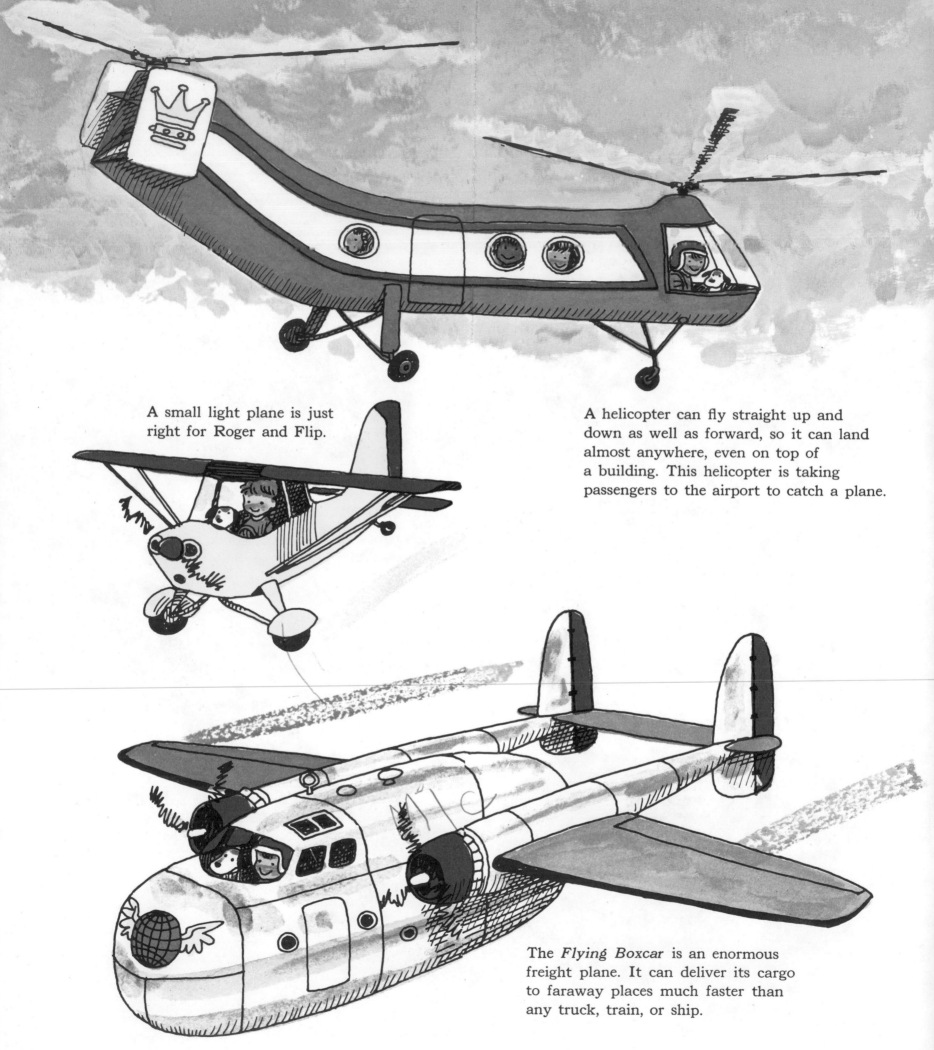

A small light plane is just right for Roger and Flip.

A helicopter can fly straight up and down as well as forward, so it can land almost anywhere, even on top of a building. This helicopter is taking passengers to the airport to catch a plane.

The *Flying Boxcar* is an enormous freight plane. It can deliver its cargo to faraway places much faster than any truck, train, or ship.

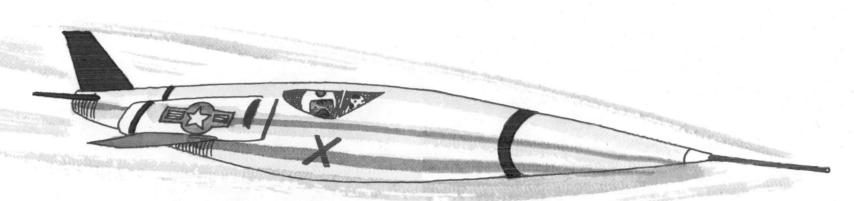

Research planes test new designs and equipment. Those brave test pilots Roger and Flip are flying this one.

Roger has invented this strange flying machine for short hops. Do you think it will work?

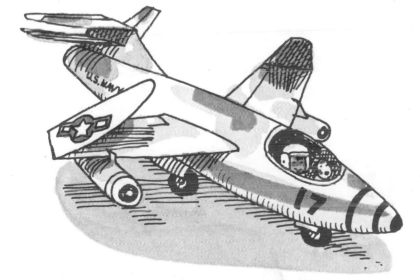

Navy aircraft carrier planes have wings that fold up when not in use. That way, many planes can be squeezed together on the deck of the aircraft carrier.

Some helicopters are so big and powerful that they can lift heavy trucks.

Astronaut Roy is orbiting the moon
in his command module. He's waiting
for the lunar module and his astronaut
friends to come back from the moon.

The Mercury space capsule carried
the first American astronaut into
orbit around the Earth. Would
you like to be an astronaut?

The Gemini spacecraft carried two astronauts into Earth orbit.

Roger, Flip, and their friend James are about to land their lunar module on the moon. What will they find there?

Trains
and
Locomotives

29

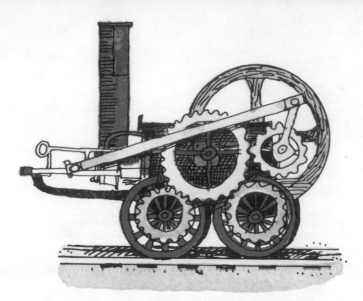

This tiny locomotive was the first
steam engine to run along railroad tracks.

The *Tom Thumb* was the first locomotive
to run in America. Early locomotives were
so slow that Flip could have beaten
any of them in a race.

Chuff-chuff. Chuff-chuff. This early
locomotive was called *Puffing Billy*
because of the way it huffed and
puffed along the tracks.

Even though this locomotive was
called the *Rocket*, it didn't go
much faster than you can run.

Sparks and smoke flew from the *Dewitt Clinton* as it pulled its stagecoach-like carriages along the tracks.

Clang-clang, clang-clang. Roger rings the *Lafayette's* brass bell as they pull into the station.

B.&O. R.R.

LAFAYETTE

This type of steam locomotive, pulling passengers and freight cars, helped to settle the American West.

Old-time locomotives were gaily painted. This is one of Roger and Flip's favorites.

Flip wants to drive this locomotive. Do you think Roger should let him?

The docksider is a special engine used
to pull freight cars along the docks
of a busy port.

The diescl switch engine is used in
railroad yards to switch cars from
one train to another.

This is a European steam engine pulling a small boxcar. What do you think is in that boxcar? Flip wishes it were full of dog biscuits.

This is a diesel engine pulling a tank car. What's in it? Is it gasoline or oil? No, it's full of good, fresh milk!

This electric locomotive gets its power from the wire overhead. The passengers are sound asleep in the sleeping car, but Engineers Roger and Flip are wide awake and alert as their train speeds through the night.

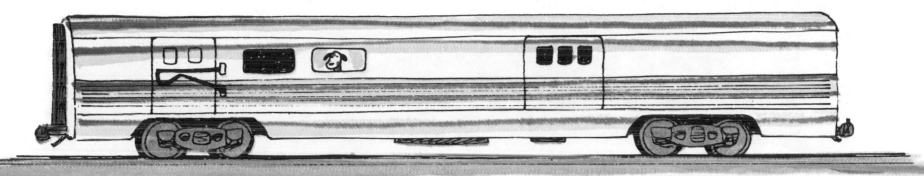

Baggage and mail cars carry baggage and letters from city to city.

Most passengers travel in a coach car.

The passengers have their meals in the dining car. I wonder what's for dinner tonight?

A dome car is a special car that gives the passengers a better view of the scenery.

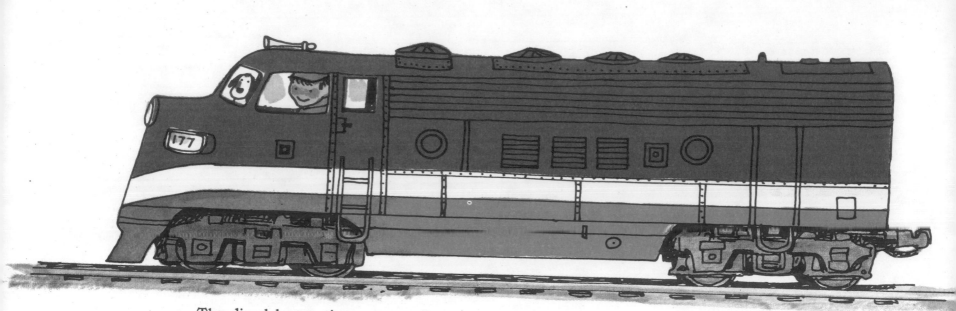

The diesel locomotive runs on diesel oil. It pulls either
freight or passenger trains.

The electric locomotive doesn't give off any smoke, so it
is used around big cities and where there are long tunnels.
Here comes a tunnel now. Pull in your head, Flip!

This passenger car has its own motor and is used for short runs.
Engineer Roger sits in the front compartment.

Roger and Flip take their friends up the mountain on the rack railway. The engine's toothed wheel fits into a toothed rail and pulls the train up the mountain.

Monorails are the newest kind of passenger train. Flip loves to whiz along above the ground. Would you like to ride on a monorail?

42 ND ST.

In the city, Roger and Flip take the subway. It rumbles through tunnels underneath the city streets.

Ships
and
Boats

The first boat was probably a raft, made by tying a bunch of sticks together. Do you think you could make a raft?

The Phoenicians were the first great seafaring people.

Ships like this sailed the Nile River thousands of years ago. They had a sail to catch the wind, and an oar for steering.

Roger, bold Viking Prince, sails the ocean in his Viking ship.

This early Greek warship had a sail and oarsmen, too. The shields protected the rowers during battle. Flip is the lookout in the forecastle.

Ships with many masts and sails could travel to faraway places. Christopher Columbus sailed the *Santa Maria* from Spain to America.

The Pilgrims sailed to America on the *Mayflower*.

"Yo ho ho," sing the desperate pirates, as they search the high seas for treasure ships to rob.

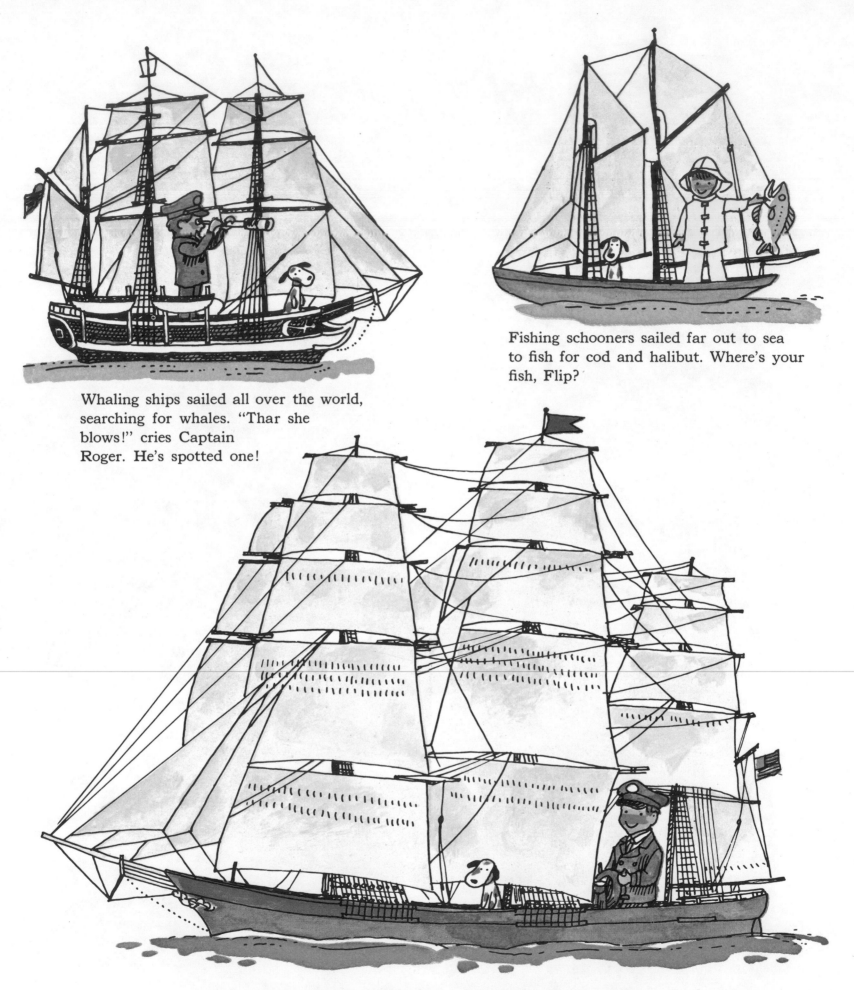

Whaling ships sailed all over the world, searching for whales. "Thar she blows!" cries Captain Roger. He's spotted one!

Fishing schooners sailed far out to sea to fish for cod and halibut. Where's your fish, Flip?

Clipper ships were the fastest and most beautiful sailing ships. They carried cargo to and from ports all over the world.

If you lived in a houseboat, you could float from place to place and always be at home.

Aarrrr**OOOOO**. Siren screaming, the speedy police boat rushes to help anyone who is in trouble on the water.

"Be careful where you squirt that hose," says Flip.

Fireboats put out fires on other boats and docks.

Where there are no bridges, a ferryboat carries passengers and cars from one shore to another. This ferry is double-ended, so it doesn't have to turn around as it goes back and forth across the water. Do you get to steer going back, Flip?

A tanker has many tanks for carrying oil. Later, the oil
is used to make our cars go.

Cargo ships sail all over the world, taking on cargo in one port
and delivering it to another. The cargo might be food or cars
or almost anything. How about toys?

A train ferry carries trains across lakes, rivers, and channels.
The cars are rolled onto rails in the boat and tied down.

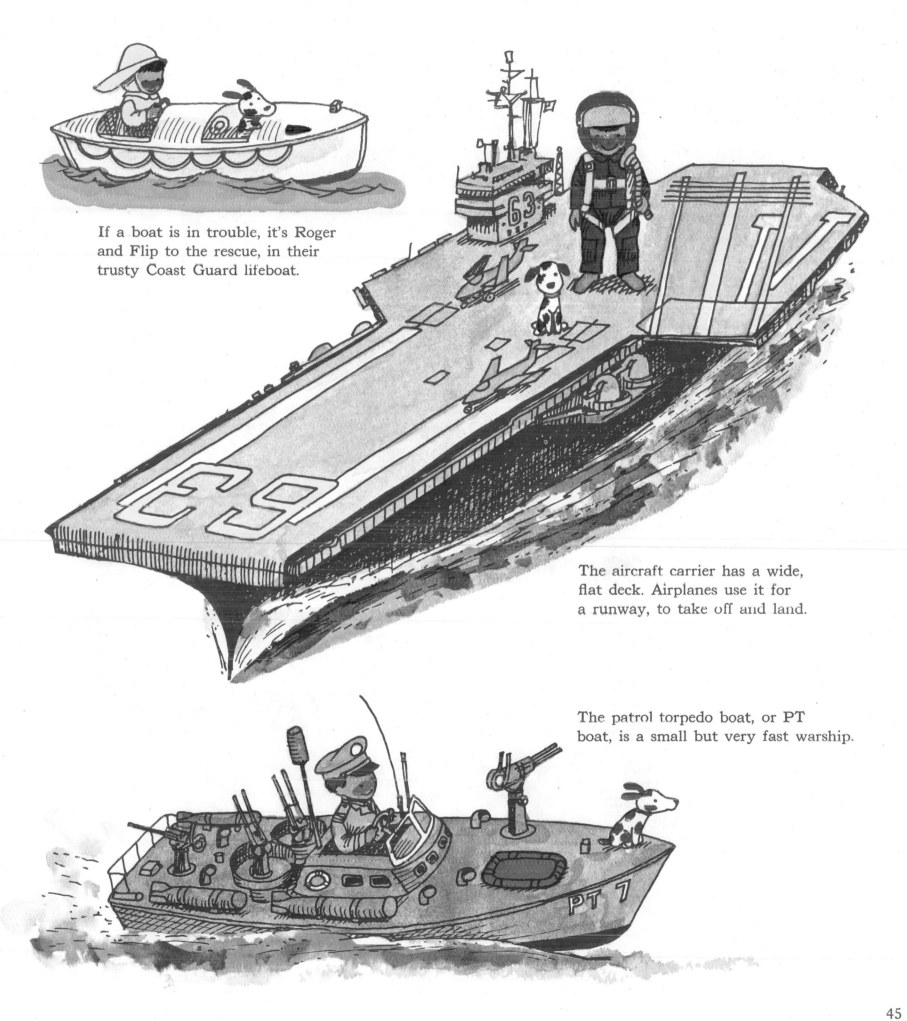

If a boat is in trouble, it's Roger and Flip to the rescue, in their trusty Coast Guard lifeboat.

The aircraft carrier has a wide, flat deck. Airplanes use it for a runway, to take off and land.

The patrol torpedo boat, or PT boat, is a small but very fast warship.

People live on an ocean liner for days as it crosses the ocean.

The hull of the hydrofoil boat rises out of the water as the boat speeds up. When the hull is completely out of the water, the boat can really speed along.

Toot, toot! whistles the little tugboat as it pulls the barge upriver. Some tugs help ocean liners to dock. Others push or pull barges. Up and down rivers, and all around the harbor, tugs are busy, day and night.

Roger puts his net over the side of his
fishing boat. When he and Flip haul it
back in, it will be full of fish—they hope!

Submarines can sail on the surface of the
sea, or dive deep down under it. Research
subs take scientists deep underwater to
study sea life. What strange deepsea fish
do you see, Flip? Not a sea monster, I hope!

Some boats are just-for-fun boats.
Roger uses his little rowboat to
explore the ponds and streams near his house.

A sport fishing boat is used for
deep-sea fishing. Did you catch
anything this time, Flip?

The outboard motorboat
speeds over the waves.

The racing boat skims the top
of the water. Flip likes to
feel the spray on his ears.

This large cabin cruiser has bunks
and a kitchen. On long trips, Roger
and Flip eat and sleep aboard.